Percy the Small

Based on *The Railway Series* by the Rev. W. Awdry

Illustrations by *Robin Davies and Creative Design*

EGMONT

EGMONT

We bring stories to life

First published in Great Britain 2004
This edition published in 2011
by Egmont UK Limited
The Yellow Building, 1 Nicholas Road, London W11 4AN

Thomas the Tank Engine & Friends™

CREATED BY BRITT ALLCROFT

Based on the Railway Series by the Reverend W Awdry
© 2011 Gullane (Thomas) LLC. A HIT Entertainment company.
Thomas the Tank Engine & Friends and Thomas & Friends are trademarks of Gullane (Thomas) Limited.
Thomas the Tank Engine & Friends and Design is Reg. U.S. Pat. & Tm. Off.

HiT entertainment

ISBN 978 1 4052 3457 3
42486/42
Printed in Italy

Stay safe online. Egmont is not responsible for content hosted by third parties.

FSC
MIX
Paper
FSC® C018306

Egmont is passionate about helping to preserve the world's remaining ancient forests.
We only use paper from legal and sustainable forest sources.

This book is made from paper certified by the Forestry Stewardship Council® (FSC®),
an organisation dedicated to promoting responsible management of forest resources.
For more information on the FSC, please visit www.fsc.org. To learn more about
Egmont's sustainable paper policy, please visit www.egmont.co.uk/ethical

*T*his is a story about Percy the little green tank engine. He was very cheeky and loved playing tricks on the other engines. But one day he needed to be brave . . .

Percy loved playing tricks on the other engines. But these tricks sometimes got him into trouble.

One morning he was being very cheeky indeed. "Peep, peep! Hurry up!" he whistled to Gordon. "Your express train's ready."

Gordon thought he was late and came puffing out. But when he looked around there was only a train of dirty coal trucks!

"Ha, ha!" laughed Percy. But Gordon didn't think it was funny at all.

Next it was James' turn. Percy told James to stay in the shed because The Fat Controller was coming to see him.

James was a very proud engine, and thought that The Fat Controller must want him to pull a Special train. He stayed in the shed all day, and nothing his Driver could do would make him move.

The other engines were very annoyed. They had to do James' work as well as their own.

At last, The Fat Controller arrived. He was very cross with James. But he was even more angry with Percy when James explained what had happened.

When Percy arrived back at the Yard, The Fat Controller was waiting for him.

"You shouldn't waste time playing silly tricks, Percy!" shouted The Fat Controller. "You should be a Useful Engine."

Later that week, Thomas brought the Sunday School children to the beach. He asked Percy if he could take them home for him.

Percy thought that it sounded like very hard work. But he promised Thomas he would help.

The children had a lovely day. But by the afternoon, there were dark clouds overhead. Suddenly there was thunder and lightning, and the rain came lashing down! The children hurried to the station.

Annie and Clarabel were waiting for them at the platform. The children scrambled into the warm carriages.

"Percy, take the children home quickly, please," ordered the Stationmaster.

The rain poured down on Percy's boiler. "Ugh!" he shivered. He thought about pretending that he had broken down, so another engine would have to go instead of him. But then he remembered his promise. He must make sure the children got home safely.

Percy set off, bravely. But his Driver was worried. The rain was very heavy now and the river was rising fast.

The rain was getting in Percy's eyes and he couldn't see where he was going.

Suddenly he found himself in deep water. "Oooh, my wheels!" shivered Percy. But he struggled on.

"Oooshsh!" he hissed. The rain was beginning to put his fire out!

Percy's Driver decided to stop the train in a cutting. The Guard went to find a telephone. He returned looking very worried.

"We couldn't go back if we wanted to," he said. "The bridge near the junction is down."

They would have to carry on to the next station. But Percy's fire had nearly gone out, and they needed more wood to keep it going. "We'll have to pull up the floorboards and burn them!" said the Fireman.

Soon they had plenty of wood. Percy's fire burned well and he felt warm and comfortable again.

Suddenly, there came a "Buzz! Buzz! Buzz!" Harold was flying overhead.

"Oh dear!" thought Percy, sadly. "Harold has come to laugh at me."

Bump! Something thudded on Percy's boiler. A parachute had landed on top of him! Harold hadn't come to laugh. He was dropping hot drinks for everyone!

Everyone had a hot cocoa and felt much better.

Percy had got some steam up now.
"Peep! Peep! Thank you, Harold!" he whistled.
"Come on, let's go!"

As Percy started to move, the water began to creep up and up and up. It began to put his fire out again!

"Oooshsh!" shivered Percy.

Percy was losing steam, but he bravely carried on. "I promised Thomas," he panted. "I must keep my promise!"

The Fireman piled his fire high with wood. "I must do it," Percy gasped. "I must, I must, I must!"

Percy made a last great effort, and cleared the flood!

"Three cheers for Percy!" called the Vicar, and the children cheered as loudly as they could!

Harold arrived with The Fat Controller.

"Harold told me you were splendid, Percy," said The Fat Controller. "He says he can beat you at some things, but not at being a submarine! I don't know what you've both been doing, but I do know that you're a Really Useful Engine."

"Oh, thank you, Sir!" whispered Percy, happily.

The news of Percy's adventure soon got back to the Station. Gordon and James heard all about how Percy had kept his promise and travelled through the terrible storm to bring the children home safely. They both thought he was very brave and forgave him for all his tricks.

Percy realised that although playing tricks could be fun, it was much more important to be a Really Useful Engine!

Thomas Story Library

 Thomas

 Edward

 Henry

 Gordon

 James

 Percy

 Toby

 Toby

 Emily

 Alfie

 Annie and Clarabel

 'Arry and Bert

 Arthur

 Bertie

 Bill and Ben

Peep!
Peep!

 BoCo

 Bulgy

 Charlie

 Cranky

 Daisy

 Dennis

 Diesel

 Donald and Douglas

Duck

Duncan

The Fat Controller

Fergus

Freddie

George

Harold

Hector

Hiro

Jack

Jeremy

Kevin

Mighty Mac

Murdoch

Oliver

Peter Sam

Rocky

Rosie

Rusty

Salty

Sir Handel

Skarloey

Spencer

Stepney

Terence

Trevor

Troublesome Trucks

Victor